"HELLO READING books are a perfect introduction to reading. Brief sentences full of word repetition and full-color pictures stress visual clues to help a child take the first important steps toward reading. Mastering these story books will build children's reading confidence and give them the enthusiasm to stand on their own in the world of words."

—Bee Cullinan
Past President of the International Reading
Association, Professor in New York University's
Early Childhood and Elementary Education Program

"Readers aren't born, they're made. Desire is planted—planted by parents who work at it."

—Jim Trelease
author of *The Read Aloud Handbook*

"When I was a classroom reading teacher, I recognized the importance of good stories in making children understand that reading is more than just recognizing words. I saw that children who have ready access to story books get excited about reading. They also make noticeably greater gains in reading comprehension. The development of the HELLO READING stories grows out of this experience."

—Harriet Ziefert
M.A.T., New York University School of Education
Author, Language Arts Module,
Scholastic Early Childhood Program

For Jamie

PUFFIN BOOKS
Published by the Penguin Group
Viking Penguin Inc., 40 West 23rd Street, New York, New York 10010, U.S.A.
Penguin Books Ltd, 27 Wrights Lane, London W8 5TZ, England
Penguin Books Australia Ltd, Ringwood, Victoria, Australia
Penguin Books Canada Ltd, 2801 John Street, Markham, Ontario, Canada L3R 1B4
Penguin Books (N.Z.) Ltd, 182-190 Wairau Road, Auckland 10, New Zealand

Penguin Books Ltd, Registered Offices: Harmondsworth, Middlesex, England

First published in Puffin Books, 1989 • Published simultaneously in Canada

1 3 5 7 9 10 8 6 4 2

Printed in Singapore for Harriet Ziefert, Inc.

WHEN THE TV BROKE

Harriet Ziefert
Pictures by Mavis Smith

PUFFIN BOOKS

Jeffrey watched television
every day of the week.

Jeffrey watched on Monday...

on Tuesday...

on Wednesday...

on Thursday...

on Friday...

and on Saturday.

On Sunday
right in the middle
of a gorilla movie—

the TV made a loud "buzz!"
The picture faded and...

the screen went black.

Jeffrey's mom turned
all the dials.
But nothing happened.

On Monday Jeffrey's dad
put the TV into the car.

Jeffrey sat on the sofa.

Now he had nothing to do.

On Tuesday Jeffrey asked,
"Is the TV fixed yet?"

"Not yet," Jeffrey's mom said.
"Maybe tomorrow."

On Wednesday Jeffrey said,
"It's tomorrow.
Is the TV fixed yet?"

"Not now, Dad," said Jeffrey.
"I'm busy. Maybe tomorrow."

On Saturday Dad called,
"I'm home! Come and watch TV.
It's all fixed!"

"Nothing much," he said.

"What are you doing now?"
asked Jeffrey's sister.

"Nothing much," he said.

"What are you doing?"
asked Jeffrey's sister.

He found paint...
scissors...crayons...
and glue, too.

Then it was Friday.

Jeffrey found some boxes.

"Will you read to me?"
she asked.
"Okay," said Jeffrey.

"What are you doing?"
asked Jeffrey's sister.
"Nothing much," he said.

"Not yet," Mom said.
"Maybe tomorrow."

On Thursday Jeffrey said,
"It's tomorrow.
   Is the TV fixed yet?"

"Not yet," she said.
"Maybe tomorrow."